G000024915

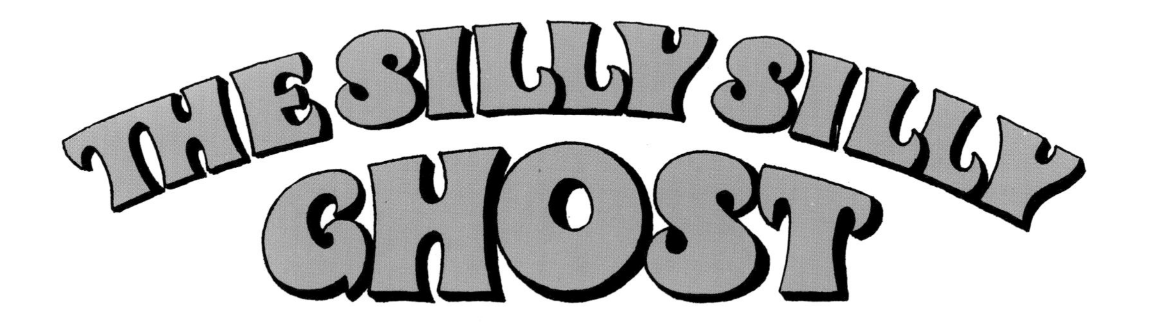

H. E. TODD

Illustrated by

VAL BIRO

HODDER AND STOUGHTON
LONDON SYDNEY AUCKLAND TORONTO

British Library Cataloguing in Publication Data

Todd, H. E.
The silly silly ghost.
I. Title II. Biro, Val
823'.914[J] PZ7

ISBN 0-340-41155-4

First published 1987

Published by Hodder and Stoughton Children's Books,
a division of Hodder and Stoughton Ltd,
Mill Road, Dunton Green, Sevenoaks, Kent TN13 2YJ

Photoset by Rowland Phototypesetting Ltd,
Bury St Edmunds, Suffolk

Printed in Great Britain by Cambus Litho,
East Kilbride

One lovely summer afternoon Bobby Brewster went for a walk. He climbed over the stile by the vicarage wall into a field which everybody called Baldwin's Field. There were some trees at the bottom of the field that he had never noticed before, so he decided to explore.

There was no wind. Everything was still and silent, with the lush green leaves drooping from their branches. Even the birds were having a siesta, sleeping in their nests. It was beautiful but rather mysterious.

Then a funny thing happened. A feeble voice behind him cried "B-o-o-o-." Bobby jumped round but there was no one to be seen.

Then the same feeble voice cried ''B-o-o-o-'' from quite a different direction, but, again, no one was there. ''What can it be?'' thought Bobby. ''No person could move so quickly as that. It must be a bird. I've heard a cuckoo call 'Cuckoo' but never a boo-bird call 'B-o-o-o-'.''

At that moment, straight ahead of him, the voice cried "B-o-o-o-" for the third time, and a grinning, fat face peeped round a tree trunk. "What a silly man," thought Bobby.

Then the man stepped out from behind the tree. He was dressed in old-fashioned clothes like those illustrated in history books.

"Good afternoon, young man," he said.

"Good afternoon, sir," replied Bobby, his eyes nearly popping out of his head.

"What are you doing in Baldwin's Wood, young man?" asked the man.

"I'm just exploring," said Bobby. "I've never been here before."

"No, I don't suppose you have," said the man. "It's not always here, and neither am I."

"Whatever do you mean?" asked Bobby. "Who are you?"
"I'm a ghost," replied the man.
"You can't be," cried Bobby. "You're far too fat and jolly for a ghost."
"That's what everyone says," sighed the man. "I was fat and jolly when I was alive, and no one will believe that I'm a fat and jolly ghost. But I will prove it to you."

He raised his arms, cried "Poopa-Poopa-Doo!" and – *PSST* – he disappeared.

"Now do you believe I'm a ghost?" cried a voice from the top of the trees.

"I certainly do," said Bobby, peering upwards.

"But you're still not frightened of me?" asked the voice.

"Not at all," answered Bobby.

"Oh dear, then I've failed again," said the voice. "So I suppose I might as well reappear."

There was a cry of
"Doopa-Doopa-Poo!"
and – *PSST* – there stood
the ghost, fatter and
jollier than ever.
"I am the ghost of Sir
Marmaduke Baldwin of
Baldwin's Castle," he
announced.
"I didn't know there was
a castle," said a surprised
Bobby.
"No, I don't suppose you
did," explained the ghost
of Sir Marmaduke
Baldwin. "Like me, it is
not always there. Follow
me and I will show it to
you."

They walked deeper into the wood, and there,
in a clearing, stood the walls of a ruined castle.

"I lived here in Baldwin's Castle, in the middle of Baldwin's Wood, for the whole of my life," said Sir Marmaduke. "And now I'm a ghost I haunt here."

"If you'll excuse my saying so, sir," said Bobby, "you're not a very good haunter."

"I know, that's my trouble," admitted Sir Marmaduke. "Everyone thinks that I'm a silly ghost. I want to be able to frighten people like a proper ghost, but it never seems to work. Why not?"

"For one thing," suggested Bobby, "you would be better dressed in ghostly white clothing."

"Very well, I'll try it," said Sir Marmaduke. "Excuse me for a minute."

He ran inside the castle and in a short time returned, wearing long white trousers and a sheet. Then he raised his arms and cried in his feeble voice: "B-o-o-o-!"
"Is that any better?" he asked.
"Not much, I'm afraid," replied Bobby. "It sounds silly when you say it like that."

"I have another idea," said Sir Marmaduke.
He took his head off, tucked it under his arm, and wandered about intoning in what he hoped was a ghostly voice: "I am the ghost of Sir Marmaduke Baldwin. I am the ghost of Sir Marmaduke Baldwin."
"How about that?" he asked anxiously.
But he looked and sounded so silly, talking from under his arm, that Bobby giggled and had to admit: "I'm afraid that was even sillier."

"Oh dear," moaned Sir Marmaduke, replacing his head on his neck. "What a silly silly ghost I am. I might just as well disappear for ever and never try to haunt again."
He raised his arms and cried: "Poopa-Doo!"
But he had left out one "Poopa" so – *PSST* – only his bottom half disappeared.
"Now I can't even make myself disappear properly," he sighed.

At that moment two rough-looking men broke through the trees towards the castle. One of them was carrying a sack.

"I've never seen these ruins before," he said to the other man. "We can hide our swag behind a wall and go back and steal some more."

"They're up to no good,
Sir Marmaduke,"
whispered Bobby.
"Now's your chance.
Haunt them as you are."

The top half of Sir Marmaduke floated over the castle wall and cried "B-o-o-o-!"
The two men stood transfixed, gazing at the ghostly top half.
"Can you see what I see?" whispered the first man, dropping his sack in alarm.
"B-o-o-o-!" repeated half Sir Marmaduke, rather louder.
"Did you hear what I heard?" whispered the other man fearfully.
"B-O-O-O-!" cried half Sir Marmaduke, louder still.
"We're being booed at by a bloke with no legs," whispered the first man.
"This place is haunted. I'm off."

And they both ran away through the trees, closely followed by the floating top half of Sir Marmaduke, gaining his confidence with each "B-O-O-O-!" as he chased them.

"Good old Marmy,"
chuckled Bobby to
himself. "He may only be
half a ghost but he didn't
half scare those men
away!"
Then he had an idea.
"I'm going to look inside
that sack," he thought.

So he did – and it was full of valuable silver objects – spoons, forks, candlesticks and trays. By then half Sir Marmaduke had returned from his chase, panting and looking as pleased with himself as a top half can look.
''Well done, Sir Marmaduke,'' said Bobby.
''Yes,'' agreed Sir Marmaduke, proudly. ''Thanks to you I'm no longer a silly silly ghost, but a really frightening one. In future I will always wear white and haunt in half.''
''That's a good idea,'' agreed Bobby. ''I'm sure it will work.''

"Well, I'll be off now," continued Sir Marmaduke. "I have enjoyed meeting you, young man. Perhaps we may meet again – but I promise to haunt you fully-dressed and all in one piece, so that you are not frightened of me."

"That is very thoughtful of you, sir," replied Bobby. "I like you best when you are fat and jolly."

"Goodbye," concluded Sir Marmaduke. "I will now complete my disappearance."

He raised his arms, cried: "Poopa-Doo!" again and – *PSST* – his top half disappeared too.

It was time for Bobby to return home. The sack was heavy but he managed to stagger with it back through the trees and across the field. As he approached the stile the vicar climbed over it, looking agitated.

"I've been robbed," he cried. "Someone has stolen all my silver."
"Don't worry, sir," said Bobby, dropping the sack at his feet. "Here's your silver."

The vicar inspected the contents of the sack.
"You are a brave and clever boy, Bobby," he said gratefully.
"It wasn't me, sir," replied Bobby modestly. "It was half a ghost."
"Half a WHAT?" cried the vicar.
"Half a ghost, sir," repeated Bobby.
"Where?" asked the vicar.
"In Baldwin's Castle, in the middle of Baldwin's Wood," explained Bobby.
"Baldwin's WHAT?" cried the vicar.
"Baldwin's Castle in Baldwin's Wood," said Bobby. "Down at the bottom of Baldwin's Field."

And he turned round to point them out but –
PSST – they weren't there any more!